J
811.6
RAS
4655481H
10|03
Rash, Andy.
The robots are coming
and other problems
B

W9-AQZ-854

HICKORY FLAT PUBLIC LIBRARY

SEQUOYAH REGIONAL LIBRARY
3 8749 0046 5548 1

and other **PROEMS**

by **ANDY RASH**

ARTHUR A. LEVINE BOOKS
AN IMPRINT OF SCHOLASTIC PRESS

PROPERTY OF
THE SEQUOYAH REGIONAL
LIBRARY SYSTEM CANTON, GA.

THE ROBOTS ARE COMING
FOR MY PARENTS

Copyright © 2000 by Andy Rash.

All rights reserved. Published by Scholastic Press, a division of Scholastic Inc.,
Publishers since 1920. SCHOLASTIC, SCHOLASTIC PRESS, and the LANTERN LOGO
are trademarks and/or registered trademarks of Scholastic Inc.

No part of this publication may be reproduced, or stored in a retrieval system,
or transmitted in any form or by any means, electronic, mechanical, photocopying,
recording, or otherwise, without written permission of the publisher.
For information regarding permission, write to Scholastic Inc., Attention:
Permissions Department, 555 Broadway, New York, NY 10012.

Library of Congress Cataloging-in-Publication Data Available
ISBN 0-439-06386-X

The book was set in 20-point Imperfect Bold.
The art was created using gouache and india ink on Arches watercolor paper.
Book Design by Andy Rash and David Saylor

10 9 8 7 6 5 4 3 2 1   0/0 01 02 03 04
Printed in Mexico · 49
First Edition, October 2000

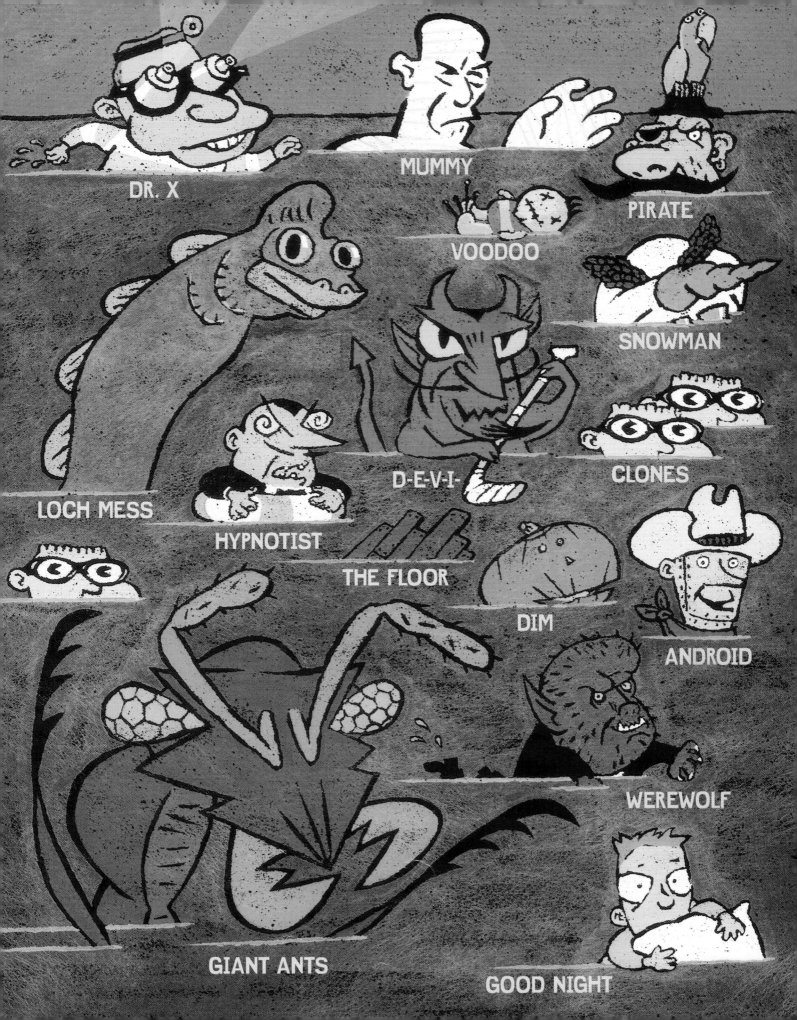

The robots are coming
right out of the lake.
They're slipping and stumbling.
They're barely awake.
They just need some coffee
poured into "intake."
Perkity, clankity, glurp.

The robots like coffee
    with sugar and cream.
They make their milk frothy
    with nozzles marked "steam."
They bake some biscotti
    with microwave beams.
Beepity, dunkity, slurp.

The robots are perking
        more mugs than required.
We'll have to start jerking
        their heads off with pliers.
The caffeine is working.
        They're totally wired.
Jittery, zappity, burp.

Dr. X has X-ray specs
and also X-ray vision.
Dr. X's dog named Rex
helped dig him out of prison.
He was jailed because he failed
to NOT see what we can't.
He has seen our bones and spleens
and bras and underpants.

The Mummy

Stumbling through
the hot Sahara
You might hear a rumbling sound.
Rumbling tummy
hungry mummy,
Hungry mummy underground.

Underground the
    mummy's cursing,
Cursing at his sandwiches.
The sandwiches
    are really hard to
Eat through all
    those bandages.

I be the bloodthirsty pirate.
And no one's as cunning as I.
I has me a peg
whar thar should be a leg
And a black patch a coverin' me eye.

I be the bloodthirsty pirate.
And no sword is faster than my.
I screwed a hook on
whar me hand is now gone
But you should see the other guy!

Voodoo

Did you do this voodoo to me?
   I feel needles on my skin.
Did you sew a voodoo doll
   and name it me and stick in pins?
Did you sneak in with some scissors?
   Did you steal some hair to keep?
And sew it on the doll and. . .
   No?
Oh well, I guess my foot's asleep.

SNOWMAN

Why not build a snowman?
A big, impressive snowman!
A cold-as-ice,
A none-too-nice,
Abominable snowman.

For his nose, shove in a carrot.
Fill his clothes with angry ferrets.
     He will learn to hum and wheeze
     With a voice box full of bees.
If you find a magic hat
Don't go near him with it, please.

In H-E-double hockey sticks
the D-E-V-I-hockey stick
just C-A-double hockey sticked
me on his special phone.

Who let the Loch Ness Monster
    in the house?
'Cause something left a slimy trail
And dripped loch water on my blouse.
Why is this house wet and messy?
I blame you, but you blame Nessie.
Who let the Loch Ness Monster
    in the house?

HYPNOTIST

I never can remember why
I do the things I do, so I
Said, "Sorry" to the girl I kissed
And blamed it on the hypnotist.

Also, I just mopped.

DIM

I'm a dim jack-o'-lantern
and I'm happy to be dim.
Other jack-o'-lanterns
burn a fire to their rim.
Their candles cook their pumpkin tops
until they shrivel up and drop
and squish their candles, snuff the light,
but my small flame can burn all night.
I'm a dim jack-o'-lantern
and I'm happy to be dim.
The brighter the jack-o'-lantern is,
the sooner the lid falls in.

android

Androids look like people.
They look just like me or you.
But inside you won't find a heart
Or any people goo.
With gears and wires, knobs and switches
They can't get rashes, don't feel itches.
Not like us, the only hitch is
Telling who from who.

The cowboys all were androids
And their faces came right off.
Oftentimes a cowboy's face
Would fall into a trough.
And then it got all bent and chewed
Because some horse thought it was food.
It's best to keep your face well glued
Or tie it with a cloth.

WANTED

BROKEN OR FIXED

The moon comes out
and the werewolf shouts,
"TIME TO BE A WOLF
AND ROAM THE FOREST!"

The moon is gone
and the werewolf yawns,
"Time to be a man
and see the florist."

The victim lies
   in the bed and sighs,
"I'll never go out
   on another full moon."

The bouquet has
   a card that says,
"Sorry I attacked you.
   Get well soon."

Giant Ants

Them giant ants are comin'.
    They been comin' here for weeks
I reckon that they got so big
    From radiation leaks.
They got too big for ant hills
    And they got too big for farms.
And one's so big he's right here
    Bitin' off my writin' arm

GOOD NIGHT

Do not be afraid to look under your bed.
These things you imagine are all in your head.
The Robots have gone and the Specs are all foggy.
The Mummy is full and the Ferrets are soggy.

The Pirate got scurvy. The Voodoo is done.
The Clones are in school multiplying by one.
The Devil is buying the Hypnotist's soul.
The Kids got a new fish and cleaned out the bowl.

The Pumpkins were made into pumpkin pie-fill.
The Floor will not hurt you if you remain still.
The Androids rode off on mechanical bulls.
The Werewolf is human (the moon isn't full).

The Ants have all scurried back into their nest.
So snuggle up tightly and have a good rest.
I'll leave the hall light on and open a crack
In the door so you'll know when the Robots get back.